RIYA SINGH

GET YOUR MOUTH READY FOR A TREASURY OF SMALL STORIES

Kathy Rather

AuthorHouse™
1663 Liberty Drive
Bloomington, IN 47403
www.authorhouse.com
Phone: 1 (800) 839-8640

Cover and interior illustration credit to Joshua Allen

Published by AuthorHouse 03/07/2019

ISBN: 978-1-7283-0254-6 (sc)
978-1-7283-0256-0 (hc)
978-1-7283-0255-3 (e)

Library of Congress Control Number: 2019902460

Print information available on the last page.

authorHOUSE®

To my son, Ryan, my constant reminder that early exposure to creative text instills a lifelong love of reading.

Get your mouth ready!

Bl
ch
Tw
Fr

bl

Bl... bl... blast out words that start with *bl*! Get your mouth ready!

During a blizzard in Bloomfield, Blake blinked his blue eyes and blushed. He blamed the blinding, blustery wind for blasting his blanket with blackberry blotches and blowing his blond hair. Bl, bl, bl!

BLOOMFIELD

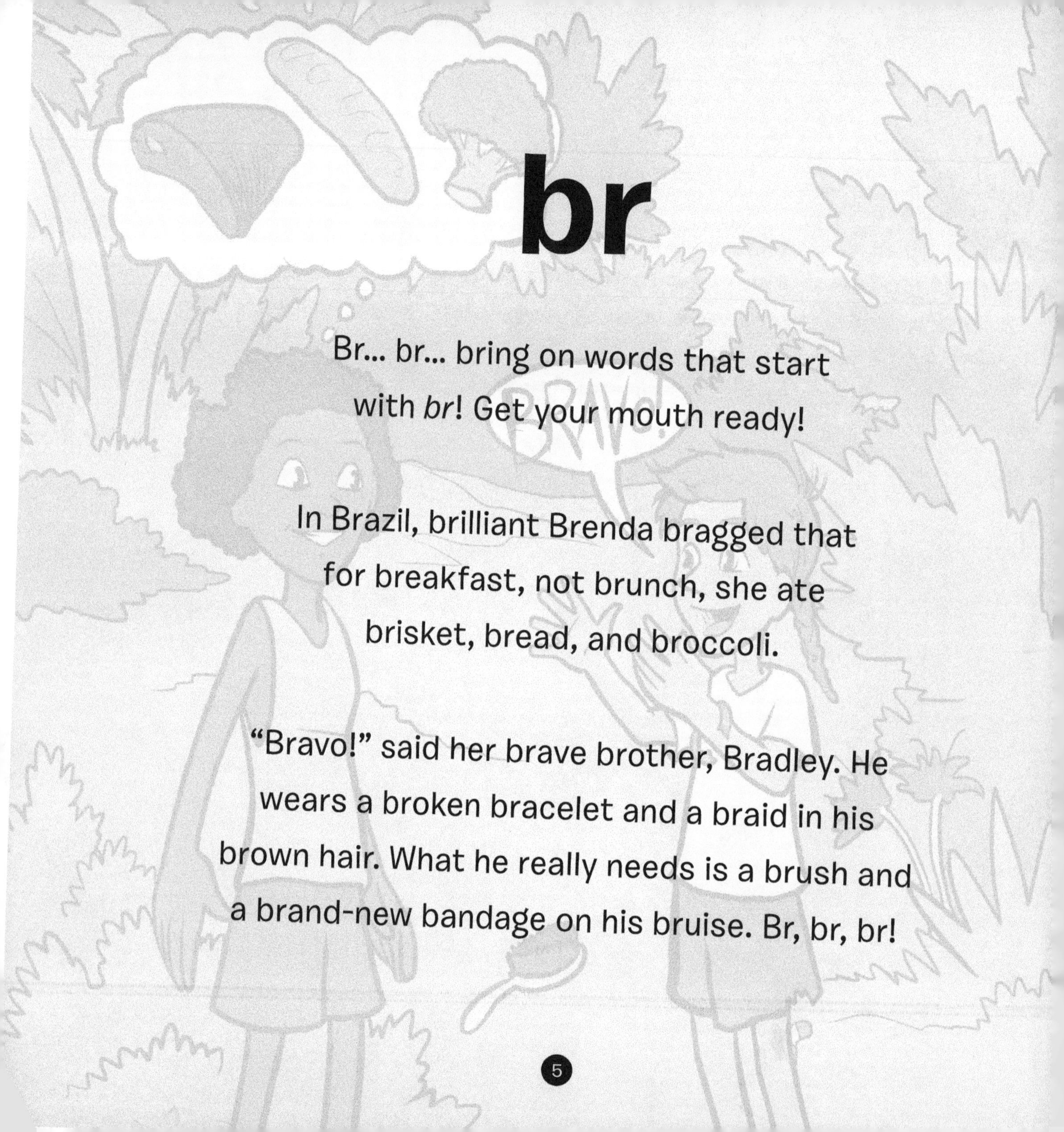

br

Br... br... bring on words that start with *br*! Get your mouth ready!

In Brazil, brilliant Brenda bragged that for breakfast, not brunch, she ate brisket, bread, and broccoli.

"Bravo!" said her brave brother, Bradley. He wears a broken bracelet and a braid in his brown hair. What he really needs is a brush and a brand-new bandage on his bruise. Br, br, br!

BRAVO!

ch

Ch... ch... choose words that start with *ch*! Get your mouth ready!

Chuck was a child when he went to China with his chinchilla. He cheered when he found a chubby chocolate chest filled with chunks of cheddar cheese, chopped chicken, and chocolate chips. Ch, ch, ch!

cl

Cl... cl... clearly name words that start with *cl*! Get your mouth ready!

On a cloudy day, clever Claire had on clean clothes. Clyde clapped and gave her a clue to close the closet in the classroom, where the clam and the clumsy clown were climbing. Cl, cl, cl!

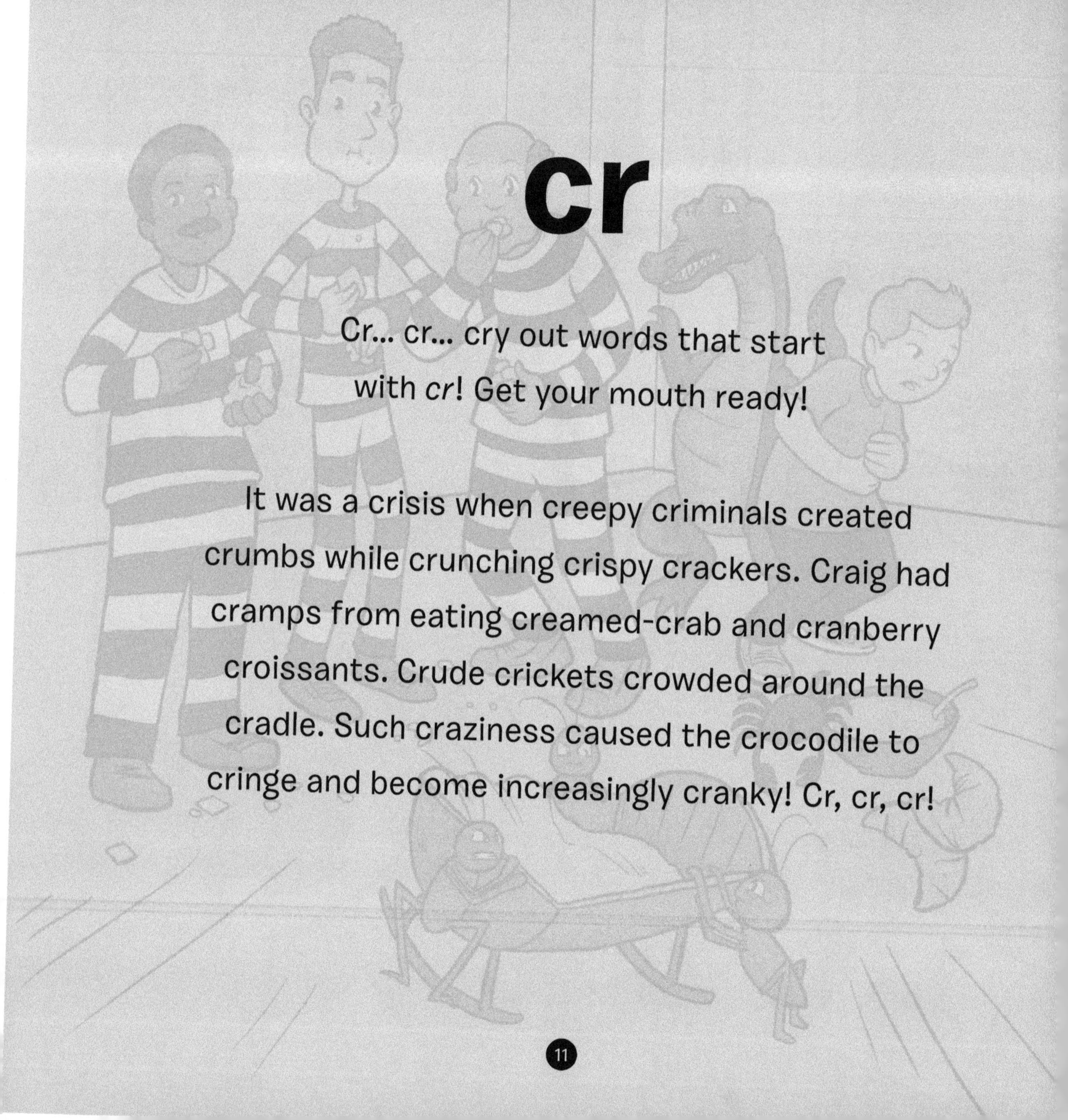

cr

Cr... cr... cry out words that start with *cr*! Get your mouth ready!

It was a crisis when creepy criminals created crumbs while crunching crispy crackers. Craig had cramps from eating creamed-crab and cranberry croissants. Crude crickets crowded around the cradle. Such craziness caused the crocodile to cringe and become increasingly cranky! Cr, cr, cr!

dr

Dr... dr... dream about words that start with *dr*! Get your mouth ready!

Drama began when a dragon in a dreadful dress nearly drowned. She was drenched, from drinking and drooling. After driving and drawing, this dreary drifter dried the drapes and dropped the drums. Oh, how drastic! Dr, dr, dr!

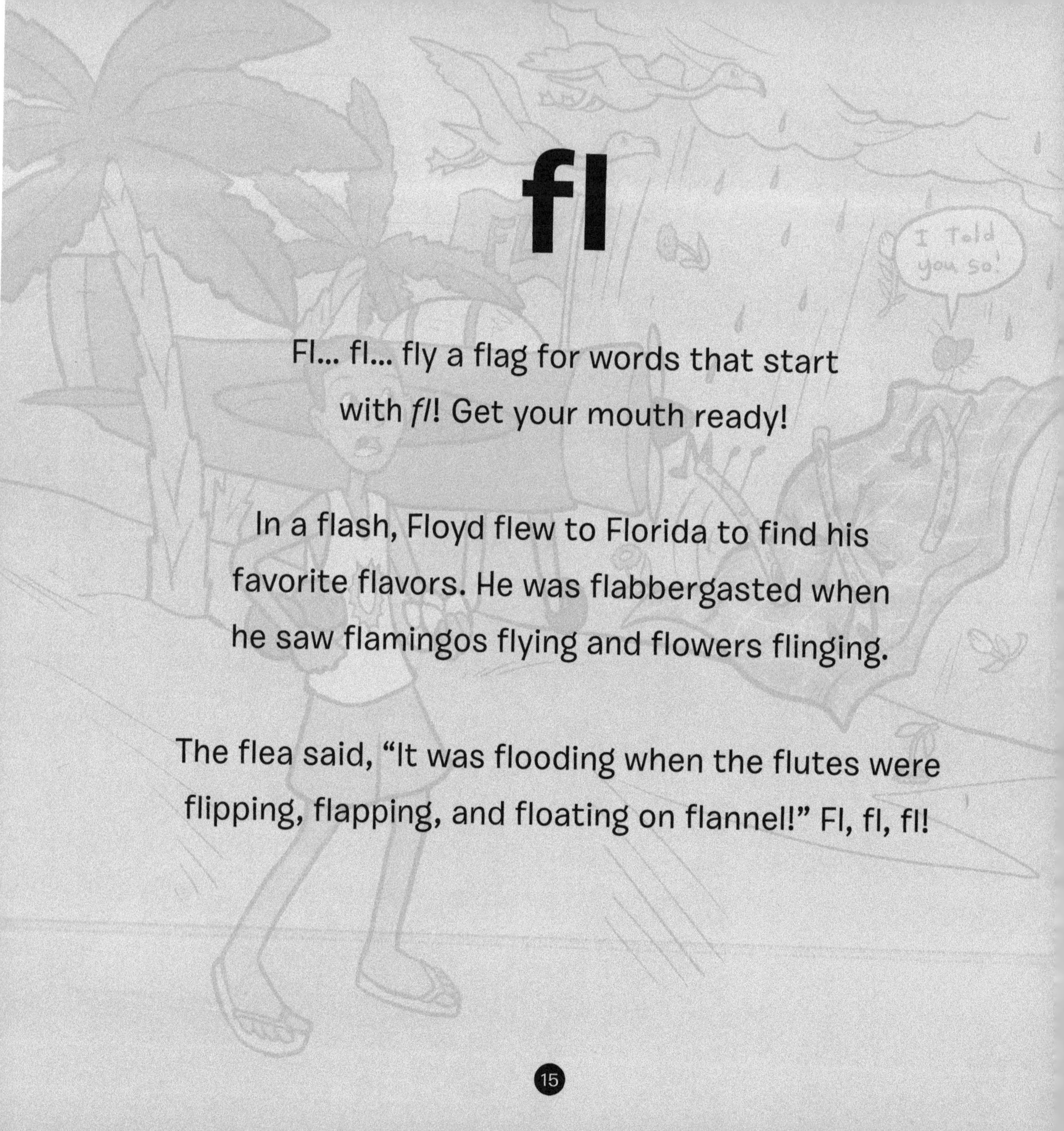

fl

Fl… fl… fly a flag for words that start with *fl*! Get your mouth ready!

In a flash, Floyd flew to Florida to find his favorite flavors. He was flabbergasted when he saw flamingos flying and flowers flinging.

The flea said, "It was flooding when the flutes were flipping, flapping, and floating on flannel!" Fl, fl, fl!

FL
I Told you so!

fr

Fr... fr... fret not about words that start with *fr*! Get your mouth ready!

In France, friendly Fred fried frankfurters, fritters, and french toast.

Frasier announced, “Don’t frown! On Friday we will eat fresh, fragrant fruit; swim freestyle; and frolic with the frisbee. We won’t be frumpy or frail!” Fr, fr, fr!

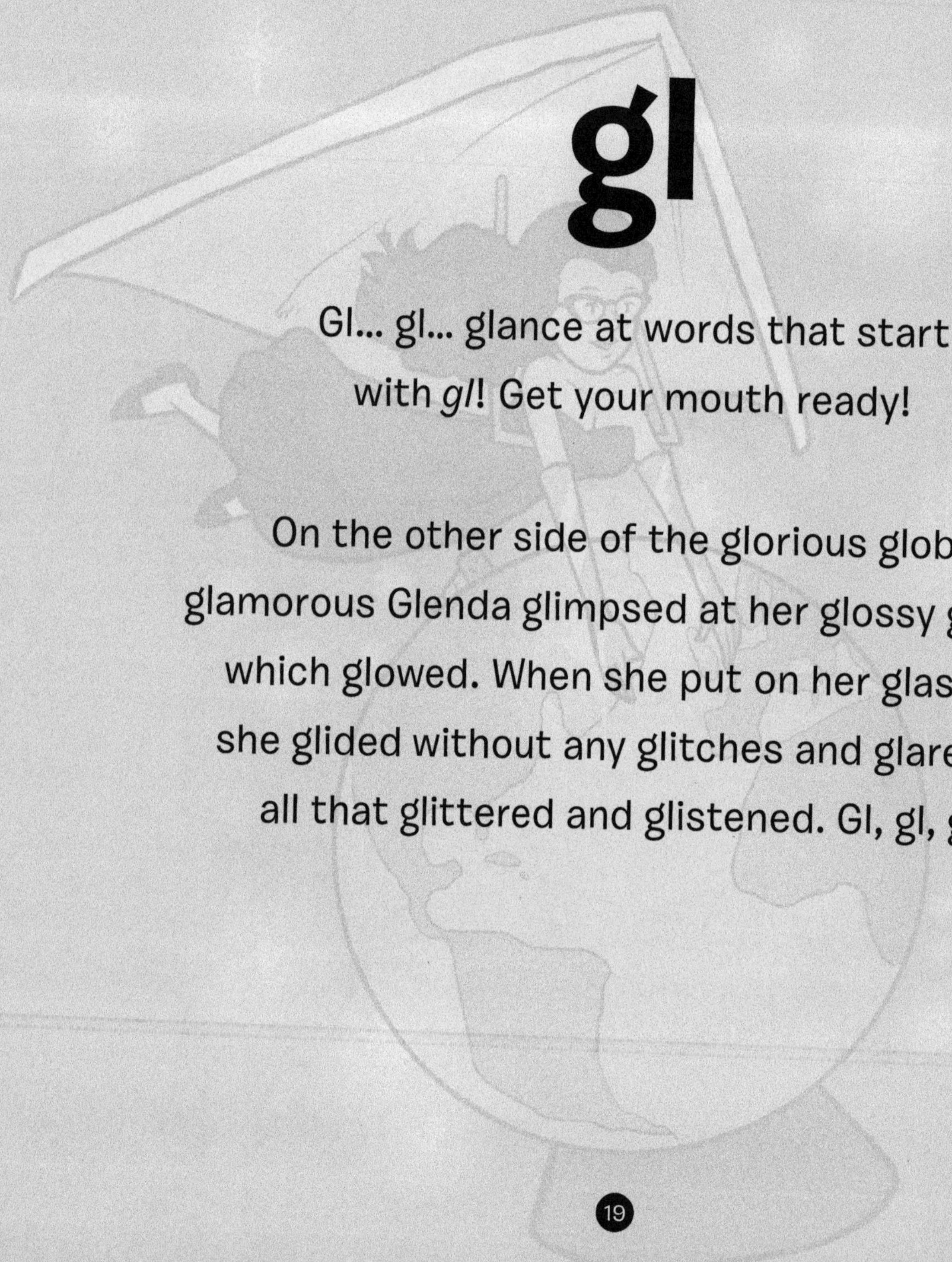

gl

Gl... gl... glance at words that start
with *gl*! Get your mouth ready!

On the other side of the glorious globe,
glamorous Glenda glimpsed at her glossy gloves,
which glowed. When she put on her glasses,
she glided without any glitches and glared at
all that glittered and glistened. Gl, gl, gl!

gr

Gr... gr... grateful are we for words that start with *gr*! Get your mouth ready!

Gretchen was greedy and gruesome! She ate gray grapes ground in greasy gravy. She growled in the green grass and grinned at the gross groom. Gr, gr, gr!

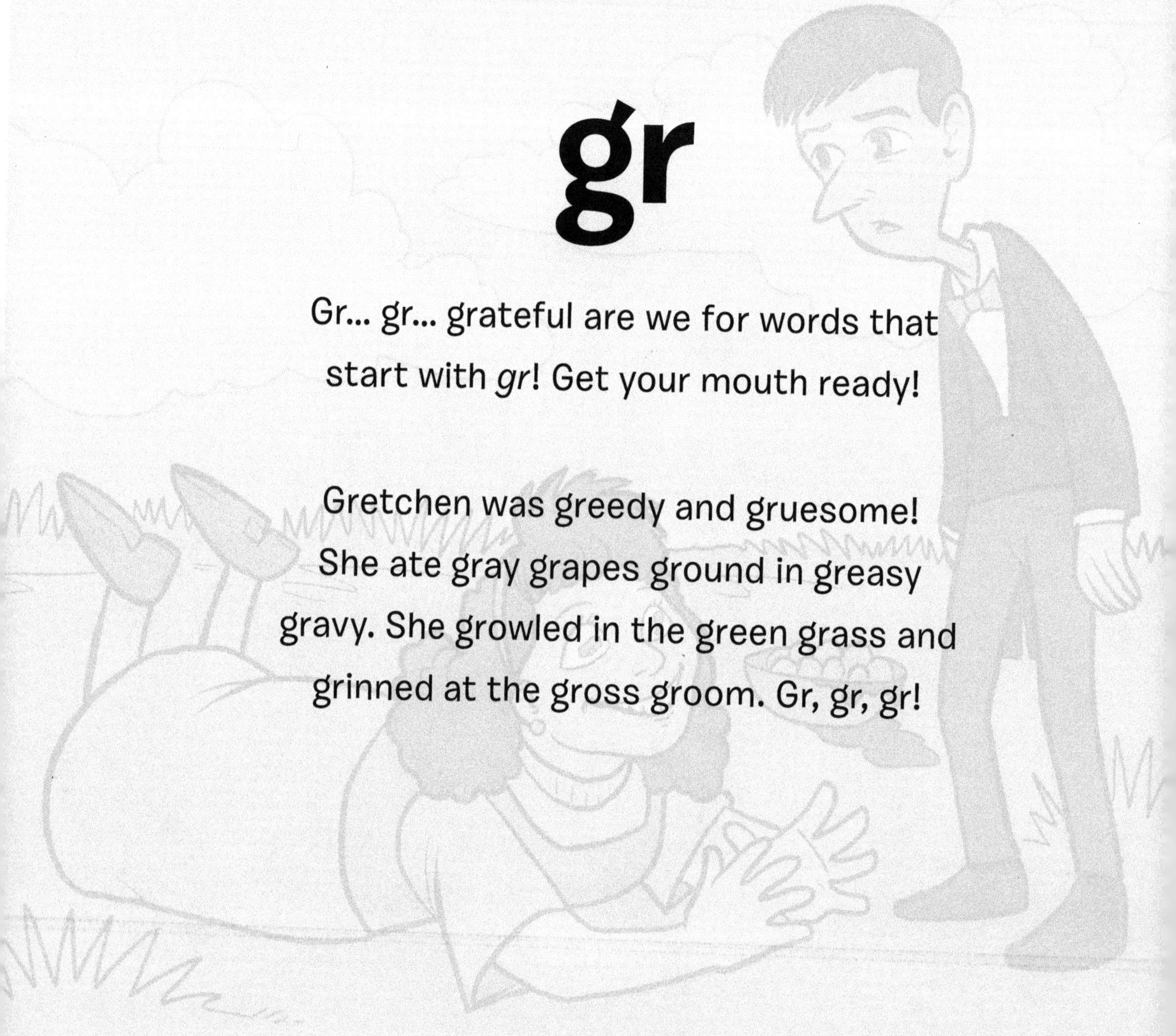

pl

Pl... pl... plenty of words start with *pl*! Get your mouth ready!

On a planet with a plethora of plums, a plumber wore a plaid shirt with plain pants. Instead of playing, he pledged that he aimed to please. He fixed the plastic plug with pliers and a plateful of plywood. Pl, pl, pl!

PLUMBER'S PLEDGE BOOK

pr

Pr... pr... practice words that start with *pr*! Get your mouth ready!

Pretty Princess Priscilla prepared the pretzels and the prunes. The practical president was probably proud when he praised her and proceeded to provide precious prizes and presents. Pr, pr, pr!

Prestigious
Pretzel
Prune
Preparer

sh

Sh... sh... shout out words that start with *sh*! Get your mouth ready!

On the shallow shore near a shapely ship, short Sherry showed shy Shannon her sharp shades and shiny shoes. They should have shopped for shells but shifted to their shelter, where they shouted at a sheep with a shield and a shaky shoulder. Sh, sh, sh!

sl

Sl... sl... slowly name words that start with *sl*! Get your mouth ready!

At the slumber party, a sleepy sloth slammed into a sled, and a sly slug slurped some slush. Then the slackers slipped on some slime while the sleeve of a slim slowpoke was slung with a slingshot. Sl, sl, sl!

sm

Sm… sm… smile when you name words that start with *sm*! Get your mouth ready!

Smug Smithers smelled smoke when his s'mores were smoldering. He was smirking when he declared, "This is not smart. There are small smears and smudges everywhere!" Sm, sm, sm!

This is not smart!
There are small smears and smudges everywhere!

sn

Sn... sn... In a snap you can name words that start with *sn*! Get your mouth ready!

The snobbish snake snickered and sneezed. So sneaky was he, snatching snacks in the snow and then snoring while snoozing.

Along came a snooping snail with a snorkel on his snout. “Instead of snitching,” he said, “let’s snuggle!” Sn, sn, sn!

ACHOO!
CHIPS

sp

Sp... sp... speak up about words that start with *sp*! Get your mouth ready!

In Spain, a spooky spider was spied spitting while speaking. Spinach was spoiled when the spicy spaghetti spilled. Now this spunky sport must spin a speckled, sparkling web in a special spot. Sp, sp, sp!

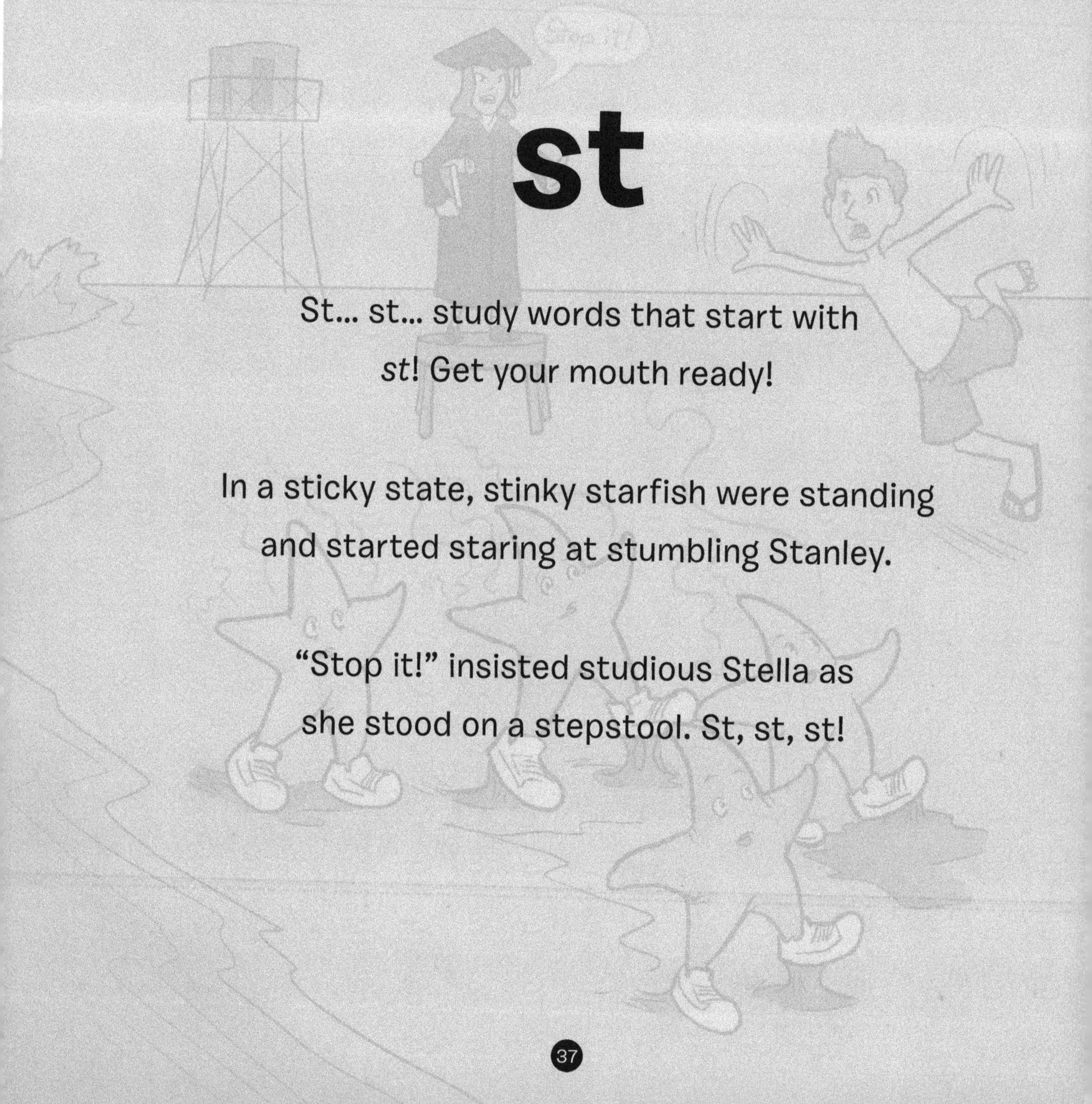

st

St... st... study words that start with *st*! Get your mouth ready!

In a sticky state, stinky starfish were standing and started staring at stumbling Stanley.

“Stop it!” insisted studious Stella as she stood on a stepstool. St, st, st!

Stop it!

SW

Sw... sw... switch to words that start with *sw*! Get your mouth ready!

Sweet Swedish swans swam swiftly on a sweltering day in Sweden. How swell it would be if they would swing without sweating instead of swimming! Sw, sw, sw!

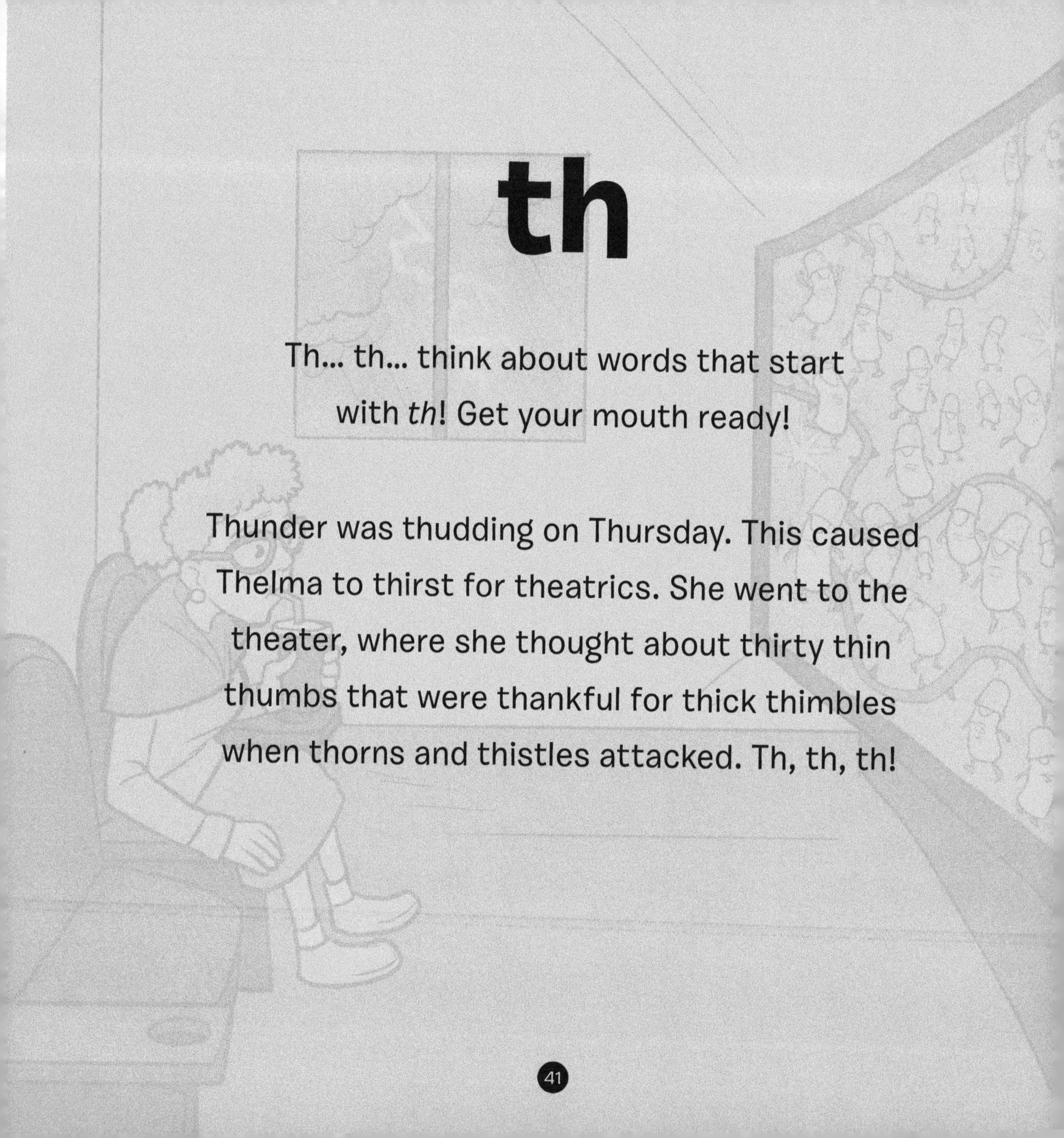

th

Th... th... think about words that start with *th*! Get your mouth ready!

Thunder was thudding on Thursday. This caused Thelma to thirst for theatrics. She went to the theater, where she thought about thirty thin thumbs that were thankful for thick thimbles when thorns and thistles attacked. Th, th, th!

tr

Tr... tr... treasure words that start with *tr*! Get your mouth ready!

Trucks, trains, and trailers traveled under tree trunks to the tropics. It is true that on this trip, tricky triplets and trim trolls trespassed. It was truly tremendous when a trombone, trumpet, and triangle trio tried to pay tribute. Tr, tr, tr!

tw

Tw... tw... tweet words that start with *tw*! Get your mouth ready!

Twelve twins wearing tweed used tweezers to twist twine. They twirled twenty times when the stars were twinkling. They twitched just twice while they tweaked their twirls. Tw, tw, tw!

wh

Wh... wh... whisper words that start with *wh*! Get your mouth ready!

Why are white whales wheezing? When will they whistle? Where is their wheel? What happened to their wheat? Which one with whiskers is whining? Wh, wh, wh!

These are my small stories, and I am sticking to them!

bl, br, ch, cl, cr, dr, fl, fr, gl, gr, pl, pr, sh, sl, sm, sn, sp, st, sw, th, tr, tw, wh

fl

br

GLUE

CPSIA information can be obtained
at www.ICGtesting.com
Printed in the USA
BVHW020212140319
542648BV00025B/312/P

9 781728 302546